THIS

by

Jamie Lee Curtis

illustrated by

Laura Cornell

Workman Publishing • New York

IS ME

A Story of Who We Are
& Where We Came From

I would like to acknowledge the ancestors — of the team at Workman and of Phyllis, Laura, and Joanna — for making their journeys and bringing these people into my life. J.L.C.

Thank you to the Cornells, Johnstons, Pells, and Littles for taking the extra journey west to the canneries in Monterey and southern California orange groves. L.C.

LIBRARY OF CONGRESS CATALOGING-IN-PUBLICATION DATA IS AVAILABLE.

ISBN 978-1-5235-0005-5

WORKMAN BOOKS ARE AVAILABLE AT SPECIAL DISCOUNTS WHEN PURCHASED IN BULK FOR PREMIUMS AND SALES PROMOTIONS AS WELL AS FOR FUND-RAISING OR EDUCATIONAL USE. SPECIAL EDITIONS OR BOOK EXCERPTS CAN ALSO BE CREATED TO SPECIFICATION. FOR DETAILS, CONTACT THE SPECIAL SALES DIRECTOR AT THE ADDRESS BELOW OR SEND AN EMAIL TO SPECIALMARKETS@WORKMAN.COM.

WORKMAN PUBLISHING CO., INC.
225 VARICK ST.
NEW YORK, NY 10014
WORKMAN.COM

PRINTED IN CHINA
FIRST PRINTING AUGUST 2016

10 9 8 7 6 5 4 3 2 1

To Jean Bennett and Deborah Oppenheimer
— J.L.C.

To my years with Jamie and Joanna,
reaching a generation in time.

— L.C.

Getting from here to there
through the ages

Blanche and Roscoe

HAPPY LIZARD

UNDER STANDING
OUR LEAST
UNDERSTOOD
PETS

ALL ABOU
CAROL
BURNETT

HOW NOT TO
GET YOUR
HOPES UP

WHAT OR
DO WE REA
NEED?

My great-grandmother came
from a far, distant place.
She came on a boat
with just this small case.

Great-Grandmother left
her family and friends,
to cross the great sea
to a land at the end.

Her parents informed her—
she had no say—

"Tomorrow we leave
for a place far away.
So fill up this case
with the things you LOVE best.
Sadly you'll have to leave
all of the rest."

Did she wear all her clothes
to leave her more space?
Could her family album
fit in this case?

I know she took ribbons

and some things to eat,

and shoes when they said
to take care of her feet.

No →    ← Yes

Her whole family tree,
pen and pencil set,
one writing journal,
a comb and barrette...

Great-Great-Grandma's necklace,
her own handmade doll
(that she clutched on her journey
when she felt very small).

How did she do it?
What would YOU take?
Would you be scared
that you'd make a mistake?

How would you know
in this case what to pack
and that once you had left
there'd be no coming back?

So you, my dear class,
have big choices to make.
When you bring this case home,
what will YOU take?

"I couldn't take paintings,
or Digglet, my rat,
or trophies, or school books,
or Dad's hand-carved bat."

"I'd take LOTS of photos and the doll my gram sewed, and my first-in-line ticket to Katy's first show."

"My punk-rocker Barbie,
'cause my mom was one, too.
My barely stuffed bear,
old Winnie-the-Pooh."

"Abuelo's beret, my ukulele,

my St. Christopher medal to look out for me."

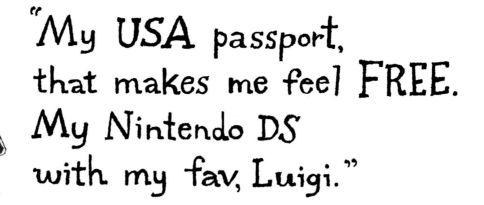

"My USA passport,
that makes me feel FREE.
My Nintendo DS
with my fav, Luigi."

"My signed Harry Potter?
My baby-tooth tin,
my aunt's high school class ring,
my dad's Navy pin."

"My Groucho Marx glasses,
 Weird Al-signed CD,
  my Notre Dame jersey,
  my karate gi."

NOTRE
DAME

"WEIRD AL" YANKOVIC
OFF THE DEEP END

"Legos, a camera
to film what I leave.
If this really happened,
it would be hard to believe."

BRIGHT
NEBULA

"But I'd be so excited
with all that was new,
people and things
to meet and to do."

Great work, Elena,
for the time that you took.
This suitcase is like
your own history book.

Elena

For who you all are
isn't JUST what you've GOT,
but part what you learn,
part what you're taught.
Who you become
STARTS with your past,
family histories
and stories that last.

This great tide that brought you,
seeds ancestors sowed,
that took root inside you
and helped you to grow.